Brave Grace

written by Pam Holden
illustrated by Kelvin Hawley

1

One day Grace saw a bat
coming out of its cave.

But she was not frightened.

One day she saw a crab
coming out of its shell.

But Grace was not frightened.

One day Grace saw a bee
coming out of a flower.

But she was not frightened.

One day she saw a snake
coming out of the grass.

But Grace was not frightened.

One day she saw a crocodile
coming out of the river.

But Grace was not frightened.

One day she saw a spider
coming out of its web.

But Grace was not frightened.

One day Grace saw a whale
coming out of the sea.

But she was not frightened.

Today Grace saw a mouse
coming out of its hole.
She was very frightened! Help!